Kids in Kitchen

Written by Jill Eggleton

Illustrated by Trevor Pye

"I am making a pizza," said Dad.

"No kids
in the kitchen!"

3

cheese

"I am slicing the cheese," said Dad.

"No kids in the kitchen!"

5

onions

"I am slicing the onions,"
said Dad.

"No kids
in the kitchen!"

tomatoes

"I am slicing the tomatoes,"
said Dad.

8

"No kids
in the kitchen!"

"I am baking the pizza," said Dad.

10

"No kids in the kitchen!"

11

"Look at this kitchen!"
said Mom.

"This kitchen is a mess!"

"This kitchen **is** a mess!"
said Dad.
"Kids in the kitchen!"

14

A Recipe

PIZZA

You will need:
pizza dough & sauce

cheese

onions

tomatoes

Put the cheese, onions, and tomatoes on the pizza.

Ask Mom or Dad to help you bake the pizza.

▬▬ Guide Notes

Title: Kids in the Kitchen
Stage: Early (1) – Red

Genre: Fiction
Approach: Guided Reading
Processes: Thinking Critically, Exploring Language, Processing Information
Written and Visual Focus: Recipe

THINKING CRITICALLY
(sample questions)
- What do you think this story could be about?
- Why do you think Dad is in the kitchen?
- Why do you think the kids want to come into the kitchen?
- How do you think Dad feels about having kids in the kitchen? Why?
- Have you ever been told to go out of the kitchen? Why?
- Look at pages 12-13. Why do you think Mom is looking angry?
- Look at page 14. Why do you think Dad is telling the kids to come into the kitchen? Who do you think should clean up the mess? Why?
- Look at page 15. What do you think this is? (recipe)
- What do you know about recipes?

EXPLORING LANGUAGE

Terminology
Title, cover, illustrations, author, illustrator

Vocabulary
Interest words: pizza, recipe
High-frequency words: I, am, no, in, the, said, look, at, this, is, a, you, will, put, and, on, get, to

Print Conventions
Capital letter for sentence beginnings and names (**M**om, **D**ad), periods, exclamation marks, quotation marks, commas